Maya & Cat

caroline magerl

WALKER BOOKS

AND SUBSIDIARIES

LONDON • BOSTON • SYDNEY • AUCKLAND

On a roof,

as wet as a seal,

as grey as a puddle,

Cat was rumbling,

a rumbly purr.

For feather boas,

she wouldn't come down ...

nor pink shoelaces

or a pompom on a stick.

So Maya sent out a boatful of fish,
under a tiny tin sail and waited
behind an open door.

Pad pad thump,
in perfectly quiet
fur boots,

Cat came to see –
and ate every
oily silver morsel!

Cat climbed high and
wrapped herself up in a soggy tail.

Maya watched her,

floating above

a thousand lit windows.

One window must be Cat's own.

Then – *pad pad thump.*

Maya placed a new can of fish
in her pocket and set out
to find Cat's home.

Cat followed politely behind.

Maya knocked on the door and asked,

"Do you belong to this cat?"

"No."

"Does this cat

belong to you?"

"No."

"Have you
lost a cat?"
"Probably not."

Cat didn't blink once

and disappeared around a corner.

Maya plodded home,

where Cat was neatly seated in her bicycle basket.

This time Maya
followed Cat's nose.
Down through the town
and across the park.

Along the shore
and onto the pier, *thunketty, thunk*
on the wooden boards.

Cat sprang

circus-lion style,

as Fritz and Irma,

beaming and calling,

threw their arms

into the air.

Cat was home.

They celebrated with teacakes

shaped like starfish.

Maya sniffed ...

just a little ...

because she would miss Cat.

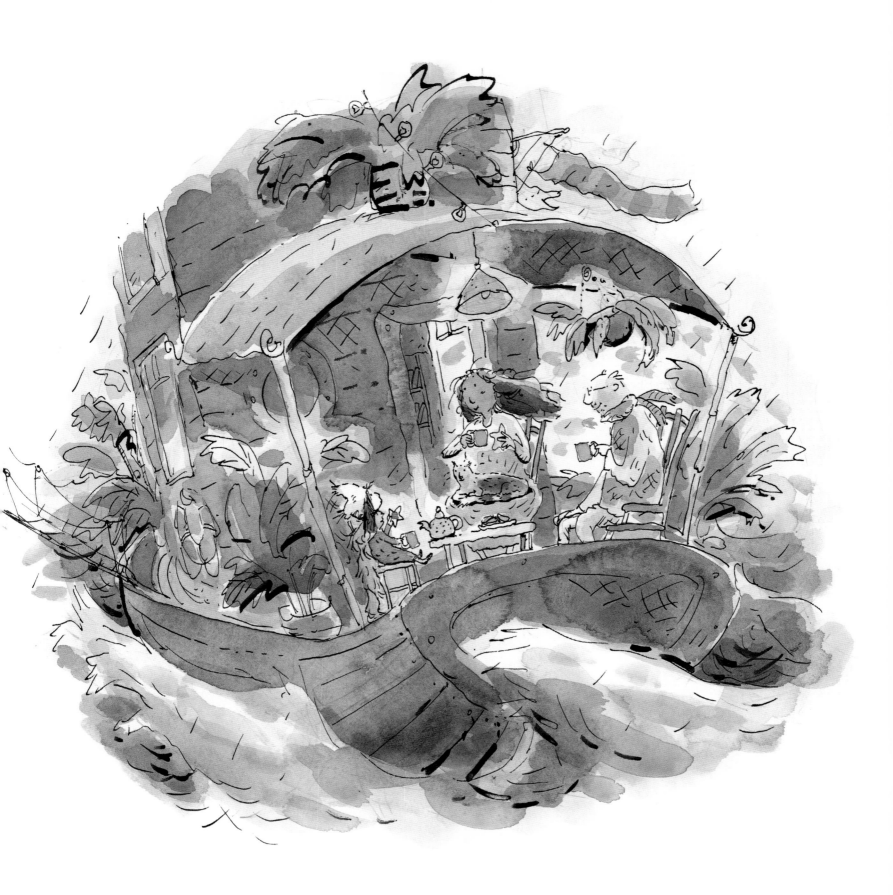

Then, sly and gentle,
Cat carried something ...

a bundle
of small and
cloudy grey ...

and gave her kitten
to Maya.

"Never seen
a kitty so seasick."
Fritz and Irma agreed.

Maya said goodbye

and rode home,

trying her best not to wobble.

That night,

the sky thundered

and the rain hosed down.

But in the waves and folds of Maya's blankets,

Moby purred a small and warm rumbly purr.